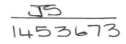

For Holly M. McGhee, Caitlyn M. Dlouhy and Emma Hughes
S. T.

First published in Great Britain 2003 by Walker Books Ltd
87 Vauxhall Walk, London SE11 5HJ

2 4 6 8 10 9 7 5 3 1

This book has been handlettered by the author

Printed in China

British Library Cataloguing in Publication Data:
a catalogue record for this book is available from the British Library

ISBN 1-84428-006-3

www.walkerbooks.co.uk

SILENT NIGHT

SANDY TURNER

WALKER BOOKS
AND SUBSIDIARIES
LONDON • BOSTON • SYDNEY • AUCKLAND

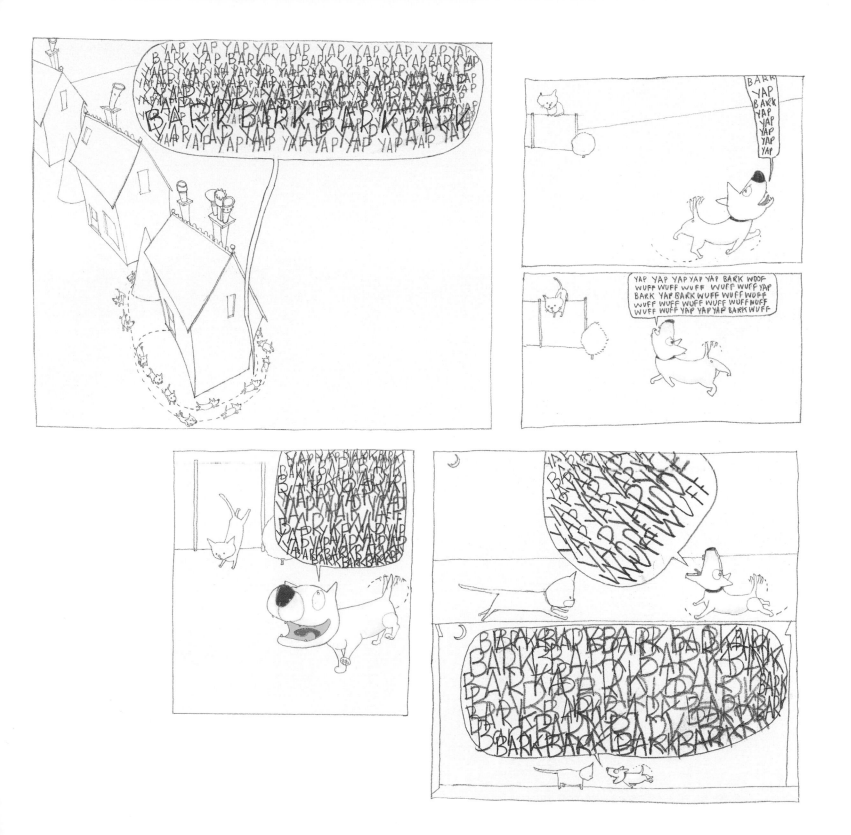